My Orange Daylily

By: Erica Mund

Thank you, grandma and grandpa, for inspiring this tale.

And thank you, Kate Hortin, for the cover you crafted.

Chapter one – 1957 Orem, Utah

Mary-Lou rolled to her side as she gazed at the blooming daylilies in her backyard. Her junior year at Orem High School had begun, and she was exhausted. Still dressed in her dance get up, grass clung to her tights, leotard, and freshly permed, brown hair. A smile stole across her face as she thought about the Tigerette's upcoming auditions and the pep club's plans for the school's Fall Dance. She was the Tigerette's cheer captain and vice chair for the pep club.

It was going to be a busy school year, but she could hardly contain her excitement as her mind raced through all the different ideas for posters and the different choreography that could be introduced.

The screen door to the backyard screeched open as her mother, Lucinda, stepped out. Lucinda kept her brown hair in style and currently sported a poodle cut. Her simple, blue dress softly accentuated her thin waist—a trait she passed on to Mary-Lou.

"Mary-Lou," Lucinda hollered, "you best finish watering those plants before daylight ends, or you won't have time for your studies."

She pushed herself up to her feet and walked over to the watering pitcher. Another smile crept onto her face as she watered her father's daylilies. Growing up as the daughter of a horticulturist, she'd grown her own love for flowers.

Orange daylilies were her favorite. A less popular color, combined with the flower everyone tended to overlook for a rose, made them an unlikely beauty. Which gave Mary-Lou all the more reason to love them.

***

Randall wiped his hands on the grease towel that hung from his jean's back pocket before pushing his wavy, brown hair out of his face. It was the last car they would service for the day before Randall split to attend his band's rehearsal.

"Mr. Wheelson, your car is ready. Your tank is full, we cleaned the windshield, and checked your tires," he said.

"Thanks Randall, give my best to your pop."

He nodded as Mr. Wheelson drove away. Randall managed his father's service station in the evenings, so he was in charge of balancing out the till at the end of the day. He wiped down the counter and quickly changed out of his service station uniform before he locked the door and left.

He hopped into his recently purchased 1951 Oldsmobile and drove down the dirt roads toward the Orem Chapel. Randall had worked hard and long to save up for his first car. His parents only ever had one car growing up, and he aimed to be independent.

The Orem chapel, where his band practiced, only sat a few blocks away from the service station. It was the only chapel in the rural area, but most of the dances they played for were held there anyways. Randall hurried through the door with the sheet music, but his plaid sleeve snagged on the door handle and ripped a whole over his elbow.

Mother can patch that later, he thought. The plaid shirt was a 5-year-old hand-me-down from his cousin. Patching it wouldn't look pretty, but it was more affordable than a new shirt.

With a gaping hole over his elbow, Randall took his place behind his drum set. His spikey-haired, blonde buddy, Brent, who played the saxophone, distributed the sheet music to everyone. That night, they were practicing the Bunny Hop by Ray Anthony.

All set up, Randall counted the band off, and they started jiving. They played at dances most weekends and made a little money. But they never made enough for Brent to save up and buy his own car.

At the end of rehearsal, Brent helped Randall pack up and haul everything out.

"Hey Randall, you know the Fall Dance is coming up, and I think we should double. I'll find a date, maybe, I dunno, the beautiful, blonde Cindy Cartwright, and you find a date, and it'll be grand. Whaddya say?

"Nah, not you too," Randall replied. "Mother keeps asking

who I'll take. If it weren't for Mr. Coxe, I'd be at college right now.

Besides, I don't dance. You'll have to find someone else to be your

ride."

Chapter Two

At the end of the first week of school, Randall sauntered into the school's main office with a few sheets of paper in hand. He tried to mask the smile that tugged at the corners of his mouth as he plopped the papers onto Mr. Coxe's desk.

Light shined through the office window and reflected off the top of Mr. Coxe's head. A stoutly man, he always preferred a sweater to a tie, not that either could hide the buttons as they stretched across his belly. His face pulled into a frown, which only accentuated the thin mustache he had been growing for months.

"Mr. Coxe, we need a parking lot guard to watch over the students' vehicles," Randall said with all the sincerity he could muster. "I have almost two hundred signatures for this petition."

Mr. Coxe looked through the petition and the signatures. He paused as if trying to read Randall's mind. Afterall, the two had a history.

During the previous school year, Randall's junior year, he had taken a chemistry class from Mr. Coxe. Randall followed Mr.

Coxe's formula to receive an A, but when he got a B+, Randall confronted him. Mr. Coxe insisted Randall was capable of more and refused to change the grade. Stuck with a B+, Randall raised mischief in the lab.

When the lab experiment required students to add 30 drops of water to change a solution's color, Randall added a half cup of water to the solution ensuring the experiment never worked. Mr. Coxe certainly had his suspicions, but he could never pin it on Randall.

So, when Randall passed Brigham Young University's entrance exam and was given a conditional letter of admittance, Mr. Coxe refused to sign Randall out of high school early.

"You have to abide by the rules," Mr. Coxe had said. "You lack half a gym credit and will have to finish out your senior year at Orem High."

Mr. Coxe shuffled through the few pages of the petition again and furrowed his brow at Randall.

"I'd volunteer to be one of the first guards on duty," Randall said. "I don't have band until third period, so another student could swap me out—that way I can attend my band and gym classes. I wouldn't want to miss gym," he added with a slight trace of sarcasm.

Mr. Coxe must have concluded that he had already won their little duel from the previous year. After all, Randall was already consigned to another year of high school.

Mr. Coxe nodded his agreement to station students as parking lot guards and went to work writing up an announcement to invite other students to guard the lot as well.

Randall had barely turned around to leave when a smirk plastered itself on his face. If he had to waste another year in high school, he might as well have the school support a pointless venture

As anticipated, sitting in the parking lot was uneventful, and it provided Randall time to read. When the toll of the bell called him back inside the school, Randall mindlessly made his way to the band room. Being six foot three, he easily looked over the top of the heads of most of the student body and could avoid shallow conversations.

Playing percussion placed Randall at the back of the classroom—where he liked to be. It was a fitting seat for a poor man's son. He was far from the front and practically unnoticeable. Sitting in the back allowed him to observe everyone around him. He could see the color rise in Cindy's cheeks when Brent winked at her. He could see daggers shooting out of the director's eyes. Randall's dance band competed against his, and, during parent teach conferences, he had complained to Randall's parents about it. But instead, his parents always encouraged Randall to keep playing.

"Hey Randall, have you given more thought to doubling at the school dance?" Brent asked after class.

Randall rolled his eyes and chuckled. "I don't know any girls I'd be interested in taking."

"Well, Cindy knows plenty of girls. She could set up one of her girl friends for you." At Randall's unconvinced face, he added,

"Come on, you know I don't have a ride to pick up Cindy. Can't you help an old buddy out?"

Randall sighed. "I dunno—"

"—I'll pay for a tank of gas."

"Alright, you got a deal."

***

"Hey James," Mary-Lou called out. "I need more glue and colored paper. Can you get some from the drawer?"

"Here they are." James Northelton handed over the requested supplies as he looked over Mary-Lou's poster. He was a tall red head, and chair of the pep club. As Mary-Lou reached for the glue, her hand brushed against his. While she paid no mind, James did.

"You know, Mary-Lou, you have a beautiful work ethic. And someone's work ethic shows in their face."

Mary-Lou tilted her head down as she raised her eyebrows. All last year, James had tried to flirt with her as he explained his own greatness.

"And a beautiful ethic such as yours deserves to be under the light of someone with my own caliber, don't you agree?"

Oh brother, she thought. *As if that line has ever swooned any girl.* "Thanks, James, but I'm not interested. I think I'll go to the dance with someone else."

Trying to hide his dejection, the bell tolled, freeing Mary-Lou from further discussion. She quickly cleaned up her materials, then ran down the hall to the girl's locker room.

Mary-Lou changed into her leotard and tights and sat on the floor while she tied her hair back into a ponytail. As she reached out to her toes, a sigh of satisfaction escaped her mouth. This was her favorite part of the day.

She started taking dance classes in elementary school and had fallen in love. She didn't' care if she was dancing alone, or dancing with a partner, dancing at all filled her with excitement and joy.

"Lou, Brent was making eyes at me in band," Cindy exclaimed as she sat next to Mary-Lou. She wore a bright pink head band to hold back her short, permed, blonde hair. She had been Mary-Lou's best friend since middle school, where they first started dancing together. "I think he might ask me to the Fall Dance. Has anyone asked you yet?"

"No one that I'll say yes to," Mary-Lou replied.

"Oh good! If Brent does ask me, I have to say yes, but I wouldn't dare go without you. If Brent asks me, maybe we could set you up on a blind date," Cindy suggested.

Mary-Lou agreed right as the bell tolled ending the school day.

Cindy hurried out of class to meet Brent by his locker.

"Hi Brent, how was schoo—"

"—Cindy, do you want to go to the school dance with me? Sorry, to cut you off, I just... I really wanted to ask you."

"Brent, I'd love to!" Cindy exclaimed excitedly.

"Great! Me and my buddy were planning on doubling, and uhh, I was wondering if you, maybe, know someone I could set him up with?"

Cindy smiled. This date was going to be absolutely perfect.

Chapter Three

On Saturday afternoon, Randall sat outside under the hot sun washing his Oldsmobile. He wanted to provide a clean, good looking ride for the evening. He spent an hour cleaning the inside until the leather seats shined. Randall figured they must have glistened in the light like that when the car was brand-new.

Randall's mother, Euveda, a plump woman, who stood at five feet and six inches, stepped outside their small home. She tucked her brown hair behind her ear as she called Randall in for supper. "The car looks lovely, now come and eat, or you won't have time to get ready."

Randall didn't go on dates often, and Euveda was excited for him to be going to a school dance. Plus, he was her oldest. She always got excited with every indication of Randall getting older.

He finished drying off the hub caps, so they reflected light better than Mr. Coxe's head, and then followed his mother inside. Randall wasn't in any hurry to get ready. After all, he was just going to wear his old, black suit.

As he walked into the house, his suit was draped across the living room chair. Euveda had just finished pressing it before she called Randall in for supper. Randall didn't wear the suit that often, but it wasn't wrinkled and didn't need to be pressed; Euveda had just wanted to make sure the suit looked its best.

Randall sat down at the kitchen table with his three younger siblings, and Debra, his younger sister, placed a pitcher of milk and a plate of bread in the center. Dinner tended to be a simple meal for the family. Randall's youngest sister, Susan, blessed the food before they ate. Randall didn't say much that evening as he didn't want to draw attention to himself.

"Randall's got a daaaate, Randall's got a daaate," sang Susan as she reached for a slice of bread.

He rolled his eyes and opted to say nothing. He knew a comment would only encourage further teasing. In his silence, his siblings dominated the conversation with their school lessons, and new favorite books.

***

"Mary-Lou, time for supper," Lucinda called.

She finished her last arithmetic question before joining the family. She had one younger sister and three young brothers, but their home provided plenty of space for them all.

"Mary-Lou, have you heard about the parking lot guards?" asked her sister, Judy as she loaded up a plate of roast beef and veggies. "Isn't that the wildest thing you ever heard?" The two sisters were a year apart but didn't float in the same social circles at school. Judy painted and wrote for the school newspaper.

"What's this about parking lot guards?" asked Lucinda. "Is someone stealing?"

"No," Judy carried on. "That's what's so crazy. A senior walked into the principal's office with a petition, and Mr. Coxe agreed."

Mary-Lou shrugged her shoulders. She hadn't heard anything about it.

"I'll bet that student is a troublemaker—probably wanted time to take a smoke at school. No respectable student would petition for such a ridiculous cause," Lucinda speculated.

Mary-Lou rolled her eyes. Mother could be quite dramatic sometimes.

***

Randall slipped off to his shared bedroom to change. His brother, Charles, was seven years younger—not an ideal roommate for a high schooler, but it was better than their last home. Five years ago, they lived in a one and a-half bedroom home. Susan wasn't born yet, but back then, Randall still shared the room with Charles and Debra.

He finished straightening his light blue bowtie in the mirror. If it didn't match her dress, he hoped his date wouldn't mind.

"I don't know when I'll be back, so don't bother waiting up," Randall said as he passed Euveda in the living room.

"Have fun and be good. Make sure you get her home on time!" Euveda called out as Randall walked out the door.

Sliding into the driver seat, he ducked his head a little extra. While he wouldn't admit it, Randall didn't want to bump his hair out of place. He revved the engine and headed down the road toward Brent's house.

Brent stood, wearing a gray suit with a soft pink bowtie, at the curb looking antsy.

"You're five minutes late," he said anxiously as he got in the car. "What if Cindy already gave up waiting and doesn't want to come anymore."

Randall shook his head. "We're fine Brent. She's probably still got her hair in curlers."

As Randall pulled up in front of Cindy's house, Brent swept up the driveway faster than Larry Jacobs, Orem High's fastest sprinter. Three swift knocks opened the door to reveal a tall, grizzly man with a thick dark mustache hiding his upper lip.

He offered no words as he stared at Brent. Just over his shoulder, Brent could see Cindy in a tea-length, pink dress with a wide skirt cinched at her waist. She flashed a smile as she approached her father's side.

"Daddy, this is Brent. I'll be back before it gets too late." Cindy reached up and gave her father a kiss on the cheek before walking out the door.

Brent, trying to not let sweat stream down his face, looked between Cindy and her father. Unsure, of what to do, he finally stammered out, "Uuuh thanks Mr. Cartwright. I'll, uuh, have her home soon."

Brent barely got back to the car in time to open the door for Cindy. Randall had watched the whole ordeal and chuckled as they slid into the backseat. He then drove around the block to Mary-Lou's house.

He pulled up and stepped out in one fluid motion.

As he walked up to the door, he thought of what to say. *Hello, I'm Randall, here for your daughter that I have never met.* He shook his head. That would make this one-time encounter awkward real fast. He rapped the door and settled to simply introduce himself.

Lucinda opened the door and eyed Randall from head to toe.

"Hello, I'm Randall—your daughters date to the dance," he offered.

"Nice to meet you, Randall. I'm Lucinda, Mary-Lou's mother. So, you go to Orem High?"

"Yes ma'am, it's my last year."

"Oooh. Are you involved in any clubs at school? Mary-Lou is involved in the pep club and the Tigerettes. She also plays a few sports. Do you play any sports?"

Oh boy, she's one of those mothers, Randall thought. *'Cuz life is only a popularity contest.* "As a matter of fact, I am the school's parking lot guard founder," he sarcastically boasted.

"Hmmm," Lucinda mumbled as disdain seared itself into every crevice of her frown. Mary-Lou walked in to view of the door, and her mother hesitantly stepped aside. Mary-Lou wore a white dress similar to Cindy's. But the blue sash around her waist accentuated the gleam in her blue eyes as she smiled.

"Hi, I'm Mary-Lou—Cindy's friend," she said as she offered her hand.

"Randall," he said as he took it and helped her through the door.

"Now, she needs to be home before dark," Lucinda advised. "I'll get bags under my eyes if I wait up any longer."

Mary-Lou quizzically looked at her mother. "Father said eleven o'clock is my curfew. I'll be back by then." She smiled softly at her mother, and then at Randall as she walked down the front porch steps.

The short car ride to the school only provided the couples time for small talk. It appeared the entire student body was arriving to the school as a pool of cars lined up in all directions, waiting their turn to enter the parking lot.

From the hallway, they could hear the live band jiving in the gym. Mary-Lou stepped towards the gym in rhythm to the music as she began to sway from side to side.

"I have to tell you, Randall, I love dancing," she said.

Randall smiled and nodded his head. "I noticed. I have to admit, I'm a lousy dancer."

Mary-Lou smiled as her eyes hinted a challenge. "No worries, I've never met a guy I couldn't teach."

"Then you must not have met many guys," Randall said.

She laughed, and they entered the gym. The gym didn't need any decorations as a sea of brightly colored dresses filled the floor. Brent and Cindy split almost immediately and began dancing.

Mary-Lou looked to Randall and offered her hand. "I assume you know the Jitterbug?"

Randall tilted his head to the side and contemplated his answer. "I know the basics."

Mary-Lou smiled again, and they began dancing. Randall stumbled over his feet a few times, but her smile never faltered.

Rather, it seemed to grow bigger each time. When he stumbled, he surprised himself by his lack of embarrassment. His elementary ability to jive was the main reason he avoided dances.

At the end of the Jitterbug, the whole crowd clapped while the band prepared to play their next song—a slow song.

"So, Randall, did you say something to my mother before I showed up?" Mary-Lou asked as they slowly swayed in a circle. "I mean, she has her own stubborn opinions of a lot of things, but usually—"

"—I told her I was the founder of the parking lot guards," Randall interrupted.

Mary-Lou mouth gaped open as she stopped for a second, but then she laughed uncontrollably as one laugh bubbled up after another. When her laughter calmed a little, she said, "My favorite flower is an orange daylily."

Randall was caught off guard. He stared at her as his brow furrowed in confusion.

"I like it because it's different," she explained. "It blooms for a day, which means most people never get the chance to recognize its full glory before it starts wilting. That makes it all the more special."

His look of confusion slowly reformed to show understanding. He let out a small laugh that stretched his smile from ear to ear. He pulled her back into his embrace as they talked and danced.

Randall relished the feeling of holding her in his arms. *I want to marry her*, passed through his mind as they swayed in sync to the rhythm.

The rest of the songs that night blurred as he could only focus on Mary-Lou. Neither of them noticed the other dancers jitterbugging and jiving while they slowly rotated in a circle.

Everyone clapped as the last song finished, startling Randall and Mary-Lou. Blood rose to her cheeks as his ears turned red. They smiled and looked around the room for Brent and Cindy. Brent and

Cindy raved about the dance and all the great music that played the entire car ride to Mary-Lou's house.

Randall walked Mary-Lou to the door in silence as a nervous excitement filled them both. At the door, he could think of nothing to say or do other than gaze into her eyes. As his smile grew, she wished the dance had never ended. He gave her a hug before leaving her in the doorway. She never wanted him to let go.

Chapter Four

A week passed, and she never heard from Randall. She never saw him at school, and she didn't dare call him. If he had been as excited as she was, he would have called by now, right? *It's probably all in my head,* she thought. *I probably just miss hanging out with Cindy.*

After the dance, Cindy and Brent began dating, so Mary-Lou didn't spend as much time with her anymore.

Lucinda, on the other hand, was pleased Mary-Lou had not heard more from Randall. She didn't want her daughter running around with a hooligan—especially not the one that petitioned for school parking lot guards.

Another week passed, and she still had heard nothing. After the football team's victory that Saturday night, she headed to Pop's Malt Shop with some friends from the Tigerettes and the football team.

Pop's Malt Shop was the biggest hangout around town. With a juke box in the corner, kids would dance in the middle of the floor. Red leathered booths lined the walls where couples and friends gathered to talk and laugh. The bar was usually reserved for the brokenhearted.

As the gang piled into the shop, Mary-Lou spotted familiar, brown, wavy hair. Randall. He sat in a corner booth with some of his bandmates, including Brent, and Cindy. Mary-Lou walked up to the counter and ordered a shake. After receiving it, she made her way over to his table.

She didn't want to join the table—not that she cared a move a like that would come off desperate, she just wanted to make a statement.

As she approached the table, everyone started scooting around to get out. *Perfect,* she thought. *This works out much better than I planned.*

Just as she got to the table, Randall slid out of the booth. "Hey Randall," she said, snapping his attention to her. "When are you going to take me out again?" A coy smile spread across her face.

Her smile soaked up his shock, allowing him to smile back. "Soon."

She smiled at her success. He gave her the response she had hoped for. *Now, I just hope that he actually calls,* she thought.

But soon never seemed to come.

At school, Mary-Lou started to pass Randall in the hall more often. *I guess I never noticed him before*, she thought. When she saw him, she'd smile and call out her tease. "Hey Randall, when are you taking me on another date?"

"Soon," he always replied.

But fall turned to winter, and Christmas break approached. Seeing Randall, and his constant response always made Mary-Lou smile, but she slowly started to think, he would never call.

The week before Christmas Break started, Brent and Cindy got into a fight over the Drifters and Buddy Holly. Cindy thought the Drifters had better music, but Brent disagreed, ending their relationship. To console her heartbroken friend, Mary-Lou suggested they go to Pop's Malt Shop.

Mary-Lou sat at the bar with her back facing the door as she swiveled to face Cindy. Cindy, to her left, cried, and Mary-Lou listened. When Cindy stopped crying, Mary-Lou tried to cheer her up with funny memories. They both started laughing as they remembered when Mary-Lou ripped her dance tights during the middle of a recital when they were ten. They hooted and hollered about pranks they played during summer camps.

Cindy leaned forward and rested her elbows on the counter. "Boys are so darn stupid."

"Yeah, they never quite do what they say," Mary-Lou agreed.

Cindy bobbed her head in agreement. She knew Mary-Lou was hoping Randall would call.

"Ya know, I thin—"Cindy's eyebrows shot up. "I-I-I think that these shakes really hit the spot. We can leave out the back and head to my house." Cindy tried to cover up for sudden reaction, but she didn't succeed.

Mary-Lou raised an eyebrow in confusion before she turned to observe whatever, or whoever, surprised Cindy.

Her eyes landed on the back of his head. The wavy, brown hair was unmistakable. Mary-Lou started to smile. *I could tease him about another da*—he was sitting alone with Jillian.

Mary-Lou sat next to Jillian in English, and they had become good friends. Jillian had said she was going on a date, but Mary-Lou never guessed it would have been with Randall.

Her head and shoulders sagged a little as she stared at the counter.

"We can still try to go out the back," Cindy suggested. "I'm sure Pop will understand."

Mary-Lou shook her head. She shouldn't feel hurt or sad. They had only been on one date, and he never called her back. In fact, this is better, right? Now she knows that he wasn't as interested, but that doesn't mean she can't still be his friend.

She shook her head again. "No, let's go out the front. I'm friends with them both. I just want to say hi."

She took a deep breath trying to inhale the confidence she wanted to present. Jillian and Randall sat at a booth near the door, and, as the two girls neared the door, Mary-Lou put on her brightest smile.

"Hi Jillian, hi Randall," she said as she walked out the door. As soon as she was out of the door, she veered to the right and walked so fast up the street Cindy had to run after her. Mary-Lou didn't want to cry. It was ridiculous to cry over a boy she barely knew. But she also felt embarrassed.

Her embarrassment became too much to hold in, so she released it in soft, hot tears. "Cindy, I wish I hadn't bothered to tease him so many times."

Chapter Five

Randall noticed a dim light emanating from the house as he walked towards the front door. *Mother must be up reading,* he thought with a chuckle. He figured Mother wouldn't notice his smile with faint light the table lamp provided. But he was wrong. In the dimly lit room, Euveda could see the shine in her son's eyes.

"Ooh hoo, looks like that dance was a fine time," she said with a chuckle. "Now, who was she? Did you kiss her? I'll bet you wanted to."

Randall's smile grew as he softly laughed at Euveda's perceptibility. "Her name is Mary-Lou. She's a junior, and she likes orange daylilies."

"And when are you taking her on another date?"

Randall dropped his head and shook it as he laughed. "Good night mother, I'll see you in the morning," he said as he stooped down to kiss her on the cheek.

"It better be soon. You don't want a nice girl slipping away," Euveda said as he walked down the hall.

He thought about calling her but wasn't sure what to plan for date. Taking her to Pop's Malt Shop felt too loud. He wanted an environment where they could talk and laugh together. A walk around town would be perfect, but what a lame date idea.

His date ideas slowly faded to the background as he continued to work long hours at the service station and play more gigs with his band. He didn't intentionally not call, in fact, he thought about calling just to let her know he was busy. But he already felt lousy getting stumped with date ideas and didn't want to prove he was lousy with a pathetic phone call.

He figured the "soon timeframe" Mother had suggested was long gone. Frustrated with himself, he decided to let Mary-Lou fade away.

Two weeks after the Fall Dance, his band headed to Pop's Malt Shop. Brent always invited Cindy to their group hangouts ever since they started dating. When Cindy sat down in their corner booth, he debated asking her about Mary-Lou. *She'd know if Mary-Lou was still interested in another date, right?* he thought.

Randall took a deep breath about to ask Cindy, but then the gang all crowded into the booth. He didn't want to ask about Mary-Lou in front of all the guys. Plus, he had already decided it was too late anyways.

But he couldn't stop thinking about her.

Every time the front door dinged, his eyes automatically flitted to the doorway. There had a been a football game that night, and he hoped she might show up.

But when Randall took the last slurp of his milkshake, he gave up on seeing her that night. The door dinged again, but he didn't bother looking. Instead, he turned his attention to the conversation. The gang was debating car models, but Randall struggled to find interest.

"Alright, well, I'm going to head home and sleep," he finally said in attempts to end the conversation.

The whole gang commented their excuses for leaving, and everyone slowly scooted out of the booth. As Randall slid out and stood up, he almost fell over.

"Hey, Randall."

It was Mary-Lou. She beamed, and it was probably because she knew she had startled Randall. "When are you going to take me out again?" Her coy smile soaked up any surprise that still clouded his mind.

It better be soon, echoed in his head. "Soon," he said as he offered a smile in return.

He had to run out the door to keep from jumping in that moment. *YES!* he screamed in his mind. *She wants another date, and I'm going give her one.*

Yet the date ideas continued to stump him. He never saw Mary-Lou at school, so waiting to call her until he had an idea would likely mean weeks of silence. He didn't want to risk his silence robbing him the opportunity for another date. So, he started walking different routes at school.

The rectangle-shaped high school halls essentially ran in a circle. Instead of heading left out of band, he started turning right.

There was never a perfect timing to when he passed Mary-Lou in the hallways. Somedays he didn't see her at all.

But when he did, she always called out her tease. "Hey Randall, when are you taking me on another date?"

Her smile always left him twitterpated. "Soon," became his constant reply. It reflected that he wanted to take her on another date, right?

A few more weeks passed, and then those weeks turned into months. At home, he tried to think of fun date that would interest her. He didn't mind taking her dancing, but he didn't want to go dancing at Pop's Malt Shop. Everybody hung around there, and they'd all comment about it the next day. While he was accustomed to negative commentary, he didn't want to subject Mary-Lou to that.

He sat at the kitchen table and decided a picnic would be a great date. They could talk and laugh, and, if she wanted to, they could even dance. He glanced out the window, and the glistening white snow reminded him of the season. A picnic would have to wait.

Euveda walked by and saw his slumped figure. "Randall, you are thinking too hard. Just take her somewhere you can both talk. I think a walk would be plenty nice."

Randall moaned. "At this point, I should call up someone else. 'Soon' has probably expired."

Euveda slowly nodded her head, but not in agreement. Randall needed to figure out dating for himself. Any mother talking her son into a date never ended anywhere good. But that didn't mean she couldn't plant ideas.

She slipped into her bedroom to jot down a few ideas. In the background, she could hear someone pick up the phone.

"Hi, this is Randall Durfey—"

She held her breath. Maybe she didn't need to plant anythi—

"—is Jillian there?"

She let out a long sigh. Jillian lived just around the block and had known Randall for a long time. She turned back to her list and plotted subtle hints.

***

The next day, Randall walked down the block to pick up Jillian. He had decided he just needed to go on another date, and he'd be able to forget about Mary-Lou. But part of him hoped a casual date would spark creative ideas.

Pop's Malt Shop wasn't too far away from their neighborhood, so they walked there. As the door rang, announcing their arrival, he immediately locked eyes with Cindy. He slowly dared to look at who she was with. Brent had told him all about their break-up, and his eyes confirmed his suspicion.

He recognized the brown, curly hair in a messy ponytail. *Beautiful,* he thought. Her hair always seemed to escape the confines of a scrunchy.

Jillian had been leading the way, so he followed her to the first booth right next to the front door. A waitress took their order, and Randall commented on the snow fall. He half listened as Jillian dove into a monologue of her love for snow. He focused on the view out of the corner of his eye.

He observed Mary-Lou glance his way and then, sag ever so slightly in her seat. *Oooh, I should have just called her,* he thought. He regretted taking Jillian to Pop's Malt Shop. He regretted letting months pass without calling her.

Randall looked at Jillian just long enough to nod his head. She must not have noticed his lack of attention as she her monologue moved onto her description of her future home. That split second was long enough for Cindy and Mary-Lou to move. He didn't where she went and didn't want to openly scan the room.

"Hi Jillian, hi Randall," Mary-Lou said.

Randall nearly jumped, and Jillian happily replied, "Hi Mary-Lou!"

Randall twisted in his seat to look at Mary-Lou, but she was already gone. He turned back to Jillian and suggest they head out. She agreed and carried the conversation on their walk home.

As they walked up her driveway, Jillian concluded, "Red roses are by far the prettiest. I mean, who doesn't love a red rose?"

Randall interrupted as he walked down the porch steps to leave. "I don't, actually. I prefer orange daylilies."

Chapter Six

Over Christmas break, Mary-Lou had come to terms with Randall not reciprocating her interest. She felt slightly embarrassed and hoped she wouldn't see him at school—avoiding any awkward confrontations. She just didn't want to wear a fake smile.

She sat down next to Jillian in English, and they started talking about the holidays.

"Sunflowers, daffodils, and daylilies," Mary-Lou named off the different flowers she helped her father plant in the green house.

"Oh my goodness, that reminds me," Jillian said. "I went on a date with Randall Durfey, and he prefers orange daylilies to red roses. Can you believe that?"

"Wait, what?" Mary-Lou couldn't believe her ears.

"That's right orange daylilies. He's such a nice guy, but he really has some strange—"

Jillian's voice faded to the background as the dance played in Mary-Lou's mind. *My favorite flower is an orange daylily.* He remembered. After so many weeks, he remembered.

***

When Randall arrived home from work that night, he noticed a vase of orange daylilies sat on the kitchen table. The image of Mary-Lou's smile as she explained her love for the flowers flashed through his mind.

"Randall, why didn't you call her?" Euveda asked. She was sitting in the corner chair reading again.

"I dunno, Mother," he said with a sigh.

"For what it's worth, I haven't seen you smile so bright since you took her to the dance."

Randall shook his head. If "soon" hadn't expired before Christmas break, it had to have by now—especially since Mary-Lou had seen him take another girl on a date. But to be fair, he didn't even enjoy the date. He was too focused on Mary-Lou the whole time.

But then, she had said hi to them both. Maybe, she was just nice, but not interested. Maybe, she was like every other a girl; a flirt that just wanted more attention.

He didn't want to play around, or flirt for fun. While most guys were interested in bingo in the backseat, Randall preferred a girl who could hold a decent conversation. He stopped walking his Mary-Lou route and turned left out of the band room.

After a few weeks, Mary-Lou still hadn't seen Randall at school, and she couldn't decide what to make of the situation.

Had he said he preferred orange daylilies because he is interested in me? she thought. *No, if he had any interest, he would have called me up. He just wants to be friends.*

She made up her mind. She'd be cordial if she saw him, and, if he ever called her up for another date, she'd go. But if not, she could still be his friend.

A few more weeks passed, but there was no sign of Randall, and Mary-Lou let him fade to the back of her mind. The sport's spring season arrived, asking the snow to leave. Mary-Lou always signed up for Tennis, and after their first practice, they all headed to Pop's Malt Shop for some team bonding.

As much as Mary-Lou loved dancing, it was nice to escape the indoors. She had convinced Cindy to join the tennis team this year, and the girls squeezed into the corner booth as they laughed out the mistakes made at practice.

Mary-Lou hadn't noticed, but Randall sat the bar. He had tried to take other girls on dates, but none had a mind quite like Mary-Lou's. None of the other girls surprised him and excited him the way she did.

He finished his milkshake right has she and her friends received theirs. With his head tilted down, he didn't notice Mary-Lou as he crossed the floor and stepped out the door. And she didn't look up as the door rang.

When Randall arrived home that night, he noticed a picnic basket sat on the kitchen table. He glanced over to Euveda, who sat in her chair reading.

"Mother, are you trying to get me to call Mary-Lou?" Randall asked.

"Oh no," she replied. "I just pulled that old basket down so I could clean it. But if you need it for a picnic date, or something, you can certainly use it."

Randall chuckled. She never was good at hiding her point. "Alright, I'll give her a call—but there's no guarantee she'll say yes."

Success, Euveda thought as she smiled.

Randall flipped through the phone book and slowly turned the dial on the phone. It rang a few times before someone answered.

"Hello?" Lucinda said through the other line.

"Hi Mrs. Rawthwort, this is Randall Durfey. Is Mary-Lou there?"

"Oh, Randall, I'm afraid she's not. She's at a friend's—"

Through the phone, Randall could hear Mary-Lou speak up. "Mother, I'm here. I can take the call, thank you."

"Hello?"

"Uuh, hi Mary-Lou, this is Randall. I just wanted to know if you were busy next weekend?"

"Hmm, let me check my calendar," she replied.

Lucinda shook her head fiercely. And through the phone, Randall could hear her whisper, "Say you're busy. He is a hooligan, and you should not go on a date."

To Randall, Mary-Lou said, "Oh how dreadful. It appears my schedule is frightfully open. What day works best for you?"

Randall smiled. "How about Saturday at noon. I was thinking of taking you on a picnic."

"Sounds lovely," Mary-Lou said as she beamed from ear to ear.

***

Randall's light blue convertible rounded the bend of the only hill in Orem. It was technically outside of town, but everyone called it Orem hill. While the snow had melted, giving room for vibrant green grass to grow, the sun was still warming up.

As they climbed out of the car, Mary-Lou hugged her arms. Ready for warmer spring days, she had failed to plan for the cooler temperatures on the hillside. Randall noticed as he walked around car to grab the blanket and basket from the trunk.

"Here," he said as he draped his jacket over her shoulders. She smiled her thanks and pulled it tight around her. Randall spread out the blanket in the sun as she took in the scenery.

Tall oak trees shaded the other side of the hill with their big green leaves. Dandelions as yellow as the sun scattered the hill side; at the end of summer, they'd be perfect for making wishes.

Mary-Lou sat down on the blanket next to Randall while he spread out the lunch he had prepared and packed. They talked and laughed as they ate. When they finished, their conversation took off as they discussed theories, hobbies, the future, and music.

Their conversation lulled, and Mary-Lou chuckled.

"After a while, I thought you weren't going to call," she said.

Randall laughed too. "For a while, I didn't think I was going to either." Randall stood up and held out his hand with a smile. "But I'm glad I finally did. Would you like to dance?"

Mary-Lou beamed back as she let Randall pull her to her feet.

They swayed on the hillside to no music, and Randall pulled her close. She rested her head on his shoulder as he said "Mary-Lou, from our first date, I think I knew dating you would mean serious commitment. I wasn't sure if I was ready for that."

She pulled her head back to look into his eyes, and he continued. "But I could never get your orange daylilies out of my head."

He pulled away and walked to the car. Curiosity filled her, and she followed. A second behind Randall, when she reached the car, he was already turning around and holding a bouquet of three orange daylilies out to her.

She laughed as she grabbed them. After smelling them, she threw her arms around Randall. "You know," she said. "You had me hooked at 'founder of the parking lot guard'."

Randall smiled as he gently cupped both of his hands behind her head and met her gaze. His eyes slowly wandered from her eyes, to her nose, to her lips. He pulled her close as he leaned in. The touch of his soft kiss melted Mary-Lou into his arms, and she kissed him back.

Chapter Seven

They were inseparable after their picnic. Lucinda heavily disapproved while Euveda couldn't have been happier. Lucinda hoped it was just a phase, and Euveda prayed for a lasting relationship.

They played tennis, went bowling, danced, and frequented the cinema. Mary-Lou came over for occasional meals at the Durfey's home, and Randall only ever picked up and dropped off Mary-Lou from her home. It was no secret that Lucinda disapproved.

As their relationship became widely known, Mary-Lou's dance instructor and high school English teacher, Mrs. Hamblin, pulled her aside after class. "Mary-Lou, do you know who you are dating?"

"I'm not sure I understand," she replied confused.

"Randall is a troublemaker," Mrs. Hamblin said. "When he took my English class, I had to have him sit in the library every day so he wouldn't disrupt. I'm just saying, you're a popular young lady and are heading great places in life. I don't want you to miss out because you got tied up with a nobody."

"Uuuh, thank you for your concern Mrs. Hamblin," she politely replied as she excused herself from the classroom.

Confusion swept over her as she left. Where had that come from? Sure, Randall had ideas that challenged tradition, but he was bright. He thought about the world in ways no one else did. She reminded herself that Mr. Hamblin was known for being a bit extreme, so she shrugged it off.

But every few weeks, another teacher pulled Mary-Lou aside to encourage an end to her and Randall. The second time a teacher pulled her aside, Mary-Lou felt she was experiencing déjà vu. But as a third and fourth expressed similar ideas, she became more confused. Mr. Coxe finally asked to speak with her on the last day of school.

"Randall has been a pretty upsetting force in many classrooms," he said. "He spent time creating a petition for parking lot guards. This boy will amount to nothing. You really should reconsider who you date."

How did so many teachers have such an opposite view than she? How could none of them see the brilliant and thoughtful mind that he possessed? Had her mother put them up to it? Had she been blinded by... by...

She couldn't bring herself to think it. They'd only been dating a few months. There was no way she could be in love. Right?

Whatever she felt, she knew she loved being with Randall. She loved their conversations. She loved his efforts to dance with her. She loved how thoughtful and caring he was. The more she let her memories of them play through her mind, the less confused she became. They didn't know him like she did. They hadn't taken the time to know him.

But she respected those teachers. She had a dear friendship with each as she worked closely with them for her clubs and sports. She'd even known Mrs. Hamblin since she started dancing in elementary school. That made it harder to disregard their opinions.

She had stopped at her locker to clean it out when Randall walked up. She still felt weighed down from all the conversations with teachers, and she hadn't told him about any of them. If she decided to end it, she didn't want things to turn nasty.

Randall noticed something was wrong from her silence and absence of a smile. "Mary-Lou, are you okay?"

She nodded to indicate she was fine, but never met his eye.

"Come on, spill it. I can see you got something on your mind."

"Randall, uuh, so many teachers have said so many things to me… about us dating… and I, uuh, I'm just trying to figure it all out," she said softly.

"What did they say?"

She sighed and shook her head. "They say you're a nobody that will only drag my potential down, but that's not what I've seen."

"Then ignore them."

Her shoulders sagged as her frustration grew. She hadn't had a chance to clear her head yet. "Randall, it's not that easy. I've known most of them for years, and I respect them."

"So, you agree with them?" he asked slowly. He had already worried that their relationship would become strained as he started college next week. He needed to clarify where she stood.

But that only seemed to aggravate the situation.

Perplexed, her tone grew agitated. "No, Randall, but I can't just ignore—I just don't know what to think." Emptiness filled her as her uncertainty grew. This was their last day together before he left. Tears threatened to fall if she stayed much longer.

"I can't do this right now," she said. "I need to clear my head so I can think." She needed space. She worried that being with Randall would sway what she felt, but if she didn't clear her head of others' concerns, she worried she would fall prey to their opinions.

"Are you going to see me off?" Randall asked. He just wanted to spend as much time with her as he could before leaving.

So focused on holding back her tears, she snapped in response. "I need to clear my head." The look of dejection on his face made her immediately regret her sharpness. He probably just wanted to say a proper goodbye before he left. But she still needed to clear her head. She closed her locker and walked away.

Calling over her shoulder, she said, "I'll try to clear my head before you leave, but there's a lot in there right now. So, don't wait for me."

She walked home in a daze with her eyebrows bunched together. With her head down, worry consumed her. So many teachers couldn't all view him as a troublemaker if he didn't stir up trouble. But, then, why couldn't she see that side of him? So many said he'd amount to nothing, but again, why couldn't she see what they saw?

The realization that she was already home shook her out of her worries for a moment. It had rained earlier that day, and she noticed water still hung to most of the flower petals. She allowed the beauty of the moment to push out all her previous concerns.

And then she saw their orange daylilies. A soft smile replaced concerned lines as she pondered their beauty. *I like it because it's different,* flashed through her mind. And then she thought of Randall.

It blooms for a day, which means most people never get the chance to recognize its full glory before it starts wilting.

Randall.

That makes it all the more special.

Randall.

She dropped her bookbag on the front lawn and started running.

Lucinda had noticed her looking at the flowers out front. "You're in a dress, you can't run. Mary-Lou, come inside."

She let the pounding of her feet on the sidewalk drown her mother out. Randall would be leaving soon. She didn't have time to explain herself.

✳✳✳

Randall finished loading up his Oldsmobile. Mary-Lou hadn't called, nor had she shown up. He paused as he saw the orange tie Mary-Lou gave him for his birthday. He chuckled. She made him laugh and smile like no one else could.

He let out a sigh.

His mind wondered through their conversation at her locker. He wished he could understand what had her so melancholic. He wanted her to be able to clear her head and let go of the sadness that seemed to grip her, but he also wanted to see her before long distance set in.

Sure, he would try to come back most weekends, but that allowed days, or even weeks, for them to live in very different lives. His environment would change the most going to college, but Mary-Lou was popular. Most the boys would probably pounce at her for shakes at Pop's Malt Shop, or school dances, or hillside picnics.

He sighed again.

"Randall, you finished packing 20 minutes ago. Why are you stalling?" Euveda asked with a gleam in her eye.

"I uuh, I guess I'm hoping to stay long enough to see Mary-Lou."

Euveda rubbed his back. Young love was such a fickle thing. "That girl has a fine head on her shoulders. When you're back next weekend, she'll have cleared up her mind."

Randall nodded. As usual, his mother was right. He focused down the road for a moment, then looked down.

"Alright, Mother, I guess this is it." He stooped down to give her hug and a kiss on the cheek before he climbed behind the wheel.

He looked in the rear-view mirror hoping to see something, but saw nothing. He turned the ignition key, and the engine roared to life. With one last look to his mother, he pulled the car out onto the road and began his drive to Salt Lake City.

Euveda watched until his car drove out of view when a faint pounding sound came from the other end of the street. She turned to see Mary-Lou sprinting towards her. As she neared the house,

Euveda met eyes, and the sad, compassionate look in Euveda's eyes said it all.

Slowly nodding her head, Mary-Lou stopped and dropped her hands to her knees gasping for breath. She dropped her head, begging the tears to stop forming in her eyes. It wasn't like she had broken up with Randall, but she felt she messed everything up.

"Why don't you come inside," Euveda suggested. She could hear Mary-Lou's sniffles and quivered breathes.

Mary-Lou's feet remained planted on the sidewalk as she tried to shake the hollowed feeling that was closing in. She couldn't shake the feeling that Randall was disappointed, and that his disappointment and physical distance would lead to a crumbling relationship. "I'm sorry, Mrs. Durfey, it's just been a crazy last day, but I'm okay." She turned to walk back the way she came.

"Mary-Lou, when you want to talk, my door is open," Euveda offered.

Mary-Lou nodded her head as her feet guided her down the sidewalk. All ability to speak seemed to escape her in that moment.

She felt embarrassed for not seeing Randall off like they planned. She felt embarrassed to have run across town, only to miss him.

She had to know when he'd return. "Mrs. Durfey, did he say when he'll come back?" she hollered out as she turned around.

"I can't say that he did, but I'll make sure he phones you when he does," Euveda promised.

Mary-Lou nodded her thanks and continued her walk home. She let out a long sigh as her mind raced with the impossible solutions before her. She wanted to tell him that she lo.. lov… that she would miss him.

But it was impossible for her to call Randall now. Had it been any other boy her mother might have helped pay for the expensive call, but not for Randall. But, even if she could phone him, she didn't want to express how she felt over the phone.

It was impossible for her to write Randall a letter—well, at least a letter that explained how she felt. It was worse than sharing it over the phone. And what if he read the letter, and didn't feel the same way? That would hurt so much more than the embarrassment she would suffer explaining her heart in person.

She sighed again.

She would have to wait until he came back for a weekend trip.

***

Although he had been accepted to BYU in high school, Randall wanted to get out on his own. His first week at the University of Utah flew by, and he enjoyed every minute of his classes and studies. He had managed to find a job at a local gas station to help pay for school, and when he wasn't working or studying, he slept.

Since the summer term began, he hadn't thought of Mary-Lou very much. He hadn't lost interest in her; he just didn't want to remember how sad she looked. He preferred to relish their inside jokes and the memories they'd made.

He had planned to return home that first weekend, since Mary-Lou hadn't come to see him off. But his new job at the station had him working the weekends. As the new employee, he couldn't already ask for time off, plus he needed the money.

Guilt overcame him for choosing work over Mary-Lou, but he felt just as guilty choosing Mary-Lou over work.

To ease his guilt, he wrote a letter to Mary-Lou. Randall figured she would understand his work dilemma, but he couldn't bring himself to write that as his excuse for staying in Salt Lake City for the weekend.

It felt weak and lousy. It might make Mary-Lou think he was starting to drift away, and then she'd probably feel terrible. After tossing ten drafts into the trash bin, he settled to simply write about his week. He glumly signed it.

Missing you,

Randall

He couldn't think of another word to accurately describe how he felt. He couldn't let go of the guilt for working. He knew a letter would never make up for his presence, but he prayed it would get to her soon.

Hopefully it could provide some sort of explanation for his absence.

He continued his studies and soon started heading to Salt Lake City's local malt shop with his roommates. It wasn't anything like Pop's Malt Shop, but he enjoyed the comradery. Later that week, as they sat around a booth at the malt shop, one of his buddies Jimmy had swiped Randall's mail.

"Hey Randall, what's this, you got some broad writing you?" Jimmy asked. "Say, is she coming down here anytime soon, we'd love to meet her. Maybe approve the holy matrimony," he sniggered.

"Maybe we can talk a girl into to going on a date with you." Randall teased in return. His eyes hinted a trace of sarcasm as the rest of the gang hoot and hollered at his taunt.

Jimmy was typically the loudest and most obnoxious one in the gang, and Randall had wiped Jimmy's smug smile clean off. He stared at Randall trying to come up with another jest. Before he could spew one out, Randall slid out from the booth and reached

out for the letter.

"Now, gimme that." Randall said.

He walked outside to the back of the malt shop. He opened

the letter and read in silence. She was teaching dance lessons

during the summer and played tennis with Cindy when they got the

chance. She sounded so happy.

Randall smiled.

She had signed her letter with Xs and Os. What he would

have done to give her a hug and a kiss in that moment.

Chapter Eight

She propped her legs on the wall as she laid in bed. It was the weekend before the dance, and Mary-Lou had yet to see Randall since he left for Salt Lake City. As much as she appreciated the letters he sent, she couldn't shake her frustration. He always seemed to be too busy every weekend.

She recognized how responsible he was with his studies and work, but surely there could have been at least one weekend for him to slip up to Orem in the past eleven weeks.

She sighed.

Some of her frustration stemmed from the upcoming dance. All her friends had dates, and she had yet to receive any indication that he would return home for that weekend. Mary-Lou had made sure to mention the dance in the last few letters, but she probably should have been more direct.

It wasn't fair to get frustrated. He worked hard to pay for his schooling, so maybe he didn't have much money left over to pay for a road trip. She saved the thought to send some money in her next letter for later. It was a nice day, and she might as well get outside and enjoy the sun.

As she walked through the living room, the phone rang. She answered, and almost dropped the phone from surprise.

Randall was on the other end.

"You didn't tell me you were coming up," she exclaimed.

"Well, it was more of a last-minute trip," he explained. "Mary-Lou, are you busy? I'd like to take you out sometime this weekend."

She smiled. He was finally here. All the frustration she felt before washed right out the door. "What did you have in mind?"

On the other end, Randall smiled wide. He regretted that it had taken him this long to finally come back, but he was glad he had. "It's a surprise, but bring a jacket."

Randall pulled up in front of Mary-Lou's house. Not much had changed. The flowers were in bloom, and the lawn looked as green as ever. Before Randall had fully stepped out of his car, Mary-Lou ran out the door and jumped into his arms.

He swung her around and planted a kiss as he set her back on her feet.

Giddy as could be, she beamed up at him as if they had never spent anytime apart. Filled with excitement, his smile matched hers.

They talked and laughed as Randall maneuvered the Oldsmobile towards the outskirts of town. Mary-Lou recognized the route. They were headed back for their picnic spot on Orem Hill.

The leaves still flaunted their vibrant shades of green as they offered a break from the sun. The yellow dandelions had faded into a sea of white-headed wishes, but they still had a unique beauty of their own.

As she once again took in the scene, she remembered her run to the Durfey's. So much time had passed, that she had forgotten about the strong feeling she wanted to share. A part of her laughed at how embarrassed and dejected she had felt not being able to say she loved Randall.

But at the same time, she didn't feel as eager to share that with him now.

Wait, what? she thought. Have I fallen out of love? Was I ever actually in love? How am I suddenly so comfortable to *use* the word? Is this all part of the distance?

She took a deep breath. She was *finally* on a date with Randall. She didn't want worries and concerns to ruin their evening together. After this weekend she didn't know when she'd see him next, so there was no sense in spending their time together worrying.

Randall had already set up their picnic when she joined him on the blanket. Their laughter continued as they ate. Randall felt as if he had never left. As he smiled at Mary-Lou, the memory of her melancholic face flashed through his mind.

He had never asked her about that day in a letter. It didn't seem appropriate, and he wanted to be able to see her face as she answered. He didn't want to interrupt their merriment if the conversation would take a turn, but he also wanted to address it.

Their conversation came to a lull as he contemplated how to phrase the question. "Uuh, Mary-Lou, do you remember the day I left? How we talked at your locker?" he ventured.

Caught off guard, her eyebrows bunched in a curious confusion. "Yeah, why?"

Randall gulped down the saliva that was building in his mouth as his nerves started to rattle. "Well, I never really understood what had you in such a pickle. I'm curious to understand what was in your head?"

A sliver of the emotions from that day rushed over Mary-Lou as she debated how much to share. A part of her felt a little frustrated. She had already told him the confusing remarks from teachers she'd known a long time. Did he forget, or did he not understand?

"I just felt really confused with the opinions of well-respected teachers clashing with my own perception. I wanted to be sure I formed my own opinion, and that I wasn't blinded by infatuation... or love or whatever."

Randall nodded his head. He remembered her mentioning the teachers, but she had appeared so down he thought there must have been something else. Does someone else's opinion really matter that much?

Unease settled over them. Mary-Lou had noticed how he became silent and somber, but that only increased her frustration. And Randall noticed her frustration increase as she too grew silent and pursed her lips.

Neither dared speak their mind first.

After what felt like minutes, Randall finally asked, "Mary-Lou, did I upset you?"

Her sharp intake of breath said enough. She looked away from Randall. Looking at anything else in that moment would help keep her calm and composed. She felt her frustration now and then were self-explanatory. She tried to refrain from being too cross with Randall, but the longer his question hung in the air, the more frustrated she became.

"Randall, I don't know how else I can explain what I've already said. How would you feel if you were in my place?"

His confusion started to turn into frustration. Why was she getting so upset with him? In his experience, some of those teachers weren't that deserving of respect. "I probably would have ignored them. They're trained in science or English, not relationships."

He immediately regretted opening his mouth as he watched Mary-Lou's eyebrows sink over her eyes.

"Take me home. Now," she demanded.

Randall hadn't intended to infuriate her. "Aah come on, Mary-Lou, I-I didn't mean that. I wasn't think—"

"—Take me home, now," she interrupted as she walked back to his car. She opened the door and climbed inside before she slammed the door shut.

Now, Randall was starting to get furious. He took great care of that car, and she knew that. She knew he hated when people carelessly shut the doors too hard. She had to have done that on purpose.

He crumpled the blanket into a ball and tossed it into the trunk with the picnic basket. Absolutely frustrated about the car door, he had forgotten why she was mad and was happy to take her home.

On the silent drive home, the tension only grew. Mary-Lou's mind fanned over all the frustrations she had felt that morning, as well as over the last several weeks. In all that time it appeared he had never taken one second to consider why she had been so upset that day. And it was in the past anyways. Why did he have to bring that up?

Randall's frustration grew as Mary-Lou remained silent. He had at least tried to apologize, and then she slammed the door. She slammed the door. What was she thinking? Worried she might key his car if he opened his mouth again, he felt content to keep it shut. It was her fault things escalated as they had. He had mostly just asked questions to clarify.

Before he had brought the Oldsmobile to a complete? stop in front of her house, Mary-Lou already had the door open and one foot out. She swung the door shut, gently this time, and ran inside the house. Her family was in the kitchen cleaning up their supper but noticed Mary-Lou enter as she slammed the front door and raced to her bedroom.

Lucinda tried to hide the smile that pulled at her lips. This must be the end of the phase.

Tears streaked down Mary-Lou's face before she had shut her bedroom door. She launched herself onto the bed and buried her face in her pillows as she cried. She cried because she was so angry. She cried because she hated to leave things so terribly with Randall. But most of all, she cried because he didn't understand— and that made her feel foolish.

Randall sat frozen in his car as he watched Mary-Lou's exit. She hadn't bothered to say anything. He had expected her to say something before she left. Unsure of what to do, he sat in the car. Should he go and knock on the door, or should he just leave?

It was better he left.

Randall figured if he knocked on the door, her whole family would crowd around to listen, and he preferred to talk with her in private. He wasn't sure she would agree to step outside for a walk around the block. But he also didn't want to initiate the talk. Mary-Lou should. She was the one so upset she took it out on Randall's car door.

As he drove home, frustration nipped at him as he tried to console his decision to leave. He drove past Pop's Malt Shop and decided to stop for a shake.

As he walked in, he saw the old gang. After ordering a shake, he joined them, and laughed as they reminisced old times. The conversation soon turned to discuss the Fall Dance, and they all looked at Randall.

"Hey, are you coming back next weekend to take Mary-Lou to the dance?" Brent asked.

Irritation flashed at the mention of Mary-Lou. "I dunno, but probably not. I work on the weekends and barely managed to get this weekend off." He didn't want to dive into their argument, even though that was the real reason he didn't plan on returning.

Despite his attempts to hide his irritation and the distance he felt growing between them, Brent noticed. He shook his head at Randall and pulled him outside the shop.

"Fess up, how stupid were you," Brent said.

Randall's irritation spiked again. Why was he the stupid one in the argument? "All I did was ask what was wrong with her on the last day of school."

Brent raised his eyebrows in confusion, and reiterated Randall's words. "Do you realize the last day of school was forever ago?"

His irritation peaked. While Randall recognized his stupidity for putting off a visit for so long, the fact that Brent recognized it in a heartbeat infuriated him even more.

"I'm outta here." Randall stormed off and headed home. His anger had grown so much he debated heading back to Salt Lake that night. He decided to call up Mary-Lou when he got home. Their conversation would help him decide. If she was still mad, he would go back to his dorm. If she wanted to talk and was apologetic, he would stay.

As soon as he pulled up, he ran inside and grabbed the phone off the hook. He listened to it ring a few times before Judy answered.

"Judy, can you please put Mary-Lou on?" Randall requested.

A moment later, he heard someone exhale long and hard. "Hello," Mary-Lou said.

Randall held his breath. She sounded upset, but not angry. He didn't want to upset her again. "Mary-Lou, it's me. I just wanted to see how you're doing. I didn't mean to make you so upset earlier."

She took a deep breath and again exhaled long and hard. "Randall, I'm sorry too. I just got so frustrated because you've been gone for so long, and with all the letters we've written—"

She stopped herself. She'd be a hypocrite to say he could have written her about it. She had specifically not written about her feelings for him, because she wanted to say it in person.

It all made sense now.

She wasn't mad that he had asked her about the last day of school, she was mad that he had also waited to have that conversation in person and waited eleven weeks to have it. Her realization returned the anger.

"I just don't understand why you waited eleven weeks to come see me. Why you waited eleven weeks to have that conversation. Am I not important to you?" Hot tears rolled down her face. She hated how easily she cried when she got angry.

Randall was caught off guard. He had never suspected she felt insecure about their relationship. But it wasn't fair to call her insecure. She was justified to feel shrugged off, he had, after all, let the whole summer pass by without one visit.

"I'm sorry, Mary-Lou." He tried to ease his guilt by consoling her.

But she wasn't done. "And of all the weekends, Randall, why did you have to come this week. I mentioned the dance to you so many times and seeing you this week—it's frustrating that I won't have a date for my last Fall Dance."

"Well, why don't you go with Brent." Randall had snapped. Brent had been right about Randall's stupidity. But the way Mary-Lou took her own jabs at him—he had never felt more vulnerable and hurt. It felt like Mary-Lou had displayed all the guilt he felt and slowly took her time to pick apart each one. Why did she have to assume he wouldn't come back? If she had simply asked, he might have made it work.

Mary-Lou didn't know how to respond. She could hear slight traces of hurt in his voice, but he didn't have to be so harsh. She had been obvious enough in her letters. And to suggest that she go the dance with someone else made it all worse. He may as well have ended things.

Her anger and frustration bubbled up inside until finally she spat out, "Maybe I will." She hung up the phone and ran to the bathroom. She locked the door and sunk to the floor as she sobbed. She never got the chance to tell Randall she loved him, and when he came, she wasn't sure she wanted to. But now, she didn't know that she ever would.

***

As Randall hurriedly threw his clothes back into his bag, Euveda stood in the doorway. She worried that he was making a rash decision. The whole family had heard his exchange of words with Mary-Lou, and she didn't want to intervene too soon. But she knew she would have to at some point.

Randall stormed down the hallway and through the living room. Father looked up from the evening paper, and his siblings stopped their game of cards to observe the scene. He didn't notice their stares, nor did he notice his mother as she trailed after him.

When he shut the trunk door, he looked up to see her standing on the sidewalk with her arms crossed and her head slightly tilted down while her gaze seared his eyes. He had to look away.

"Mother, I—" He sighed, unsure of what to say. He knew he was acting a little harebrained, but Mary-Lou wasn't all that calm either.

"What are you doing? You let the whole summer pass, and now, you're leaving before the weekend is over? All because she expressed some frustration?"

Her tone was clear. Randall was to listen and keep his mouth shut. He looked down at his shoes, bracing for the truths that would cut deep. Mother always had a way of delivering hard facts that shut down any desires to argue.

She watched him avert his gaze. She could tell he felt guilty for not coming sooner, and she understood he probably felt frustrated that after he finally came, his first night had ended in flames. Her stance softened as she tilted her head to the side.

"Randall, do you love her?"

He snapped his head up in surprise. *I want to marry her,* flashed through his mind with the image of Mary-Lou in his arms as they danced. He'd known for a long time, but it never felt like a good time to share. He didn't want to scare Mary-Lou away with such a strong conviction either.

He sighed. "I fell in love from the first moment I held her in my arms." He slowly raised his head and met his mother's gaze.

Euveda nodded her approval. "Then, you know what to do."

Randall nodded his head as he slid behind the wheel. Euveda smiled as he started to pull away from the curb. *Once again Mother saves the day,* she thought.

But her mouth gaped open as she watched him drive pass the turn for Mary-Lou's house. She thought he was going to profess his love, not drive back to Salt Lake City.

Chapter Nine

Mary-Lou slowly stopped writing Randall, and she slowly stopped receiving letters from him. She went to the Fall Dance with Brent, and to the Halloween Dance with another guy, and to the Thanksgiving Dance with another. But despite the heartache and frustration that filled her every time she thought of Randall's visit, she couldn't shake the deep-seated love she felt for him.

She had called the day after he left to apologize and ease the tension. But when Euveda said he had left the night before, she barely hung up the phone before sobs took hold of her. But as the weeks passed, and there was still no sign of Randall, frustration replaced her heartache. He hadn't bothered to send a letter explaining his sudden departure, so why should she sit around heartbroken?

But dancing with other guys only brought the heartache back. She held the same conversation with each guy. They all loved Buddy Holly, slicked their hair back, and pulled the same moves.

At first, she didn't mind the fake yawn that got his arm around her shoulder, but by the time the third guy tried the same stunt, she stopped him mid yawn. Even their conversations felt like a memorized script.

And yet, these were the boys her teachers suggested she pursue. Mrs. Hamblin pulled her aside after class just to toss around her approval.

"You know, he's one of the top players on the [insert any sport] team," she'd say. "He'll probably play in college. You should chase that!"

These conversations only ever left her feeling stupid. She had let her stomach twist into knots over their opinions before, and it wasn't until now that she could see how naïve they all were.

Dating other guys had failed to erase Randall from her heart, so with the Christmas Dance approaching, she decided she would just have to wait until college to date again. Hopefully college could introduce her to young men with a brain.

Or Randall.

She felt foolish, but she had applied for a scholarship at the University of Utah. She knew Randall was probably already dating someone else, but she hoped that, somehow, if he saw her again, they could try another date.

Uuggh, only in my dreams, she'd constantly remind herself. She thought it would never happen, but she still wanted to at least wish for it.

***

Randall had begun applying to BYU as soon has he returned to Salt Lake City. Mother was right. He needed to show Mary-Lou he loved her, and that's what he was going to do. He was going to move back to Orem to be near her as she finished her senior year.

His plan felt fool proof, until the letters slowed down. She didn't seem as happy and enthusiastic anymore, so he felt less sure about writing her back—which took him longer to send a letter. And her responses seemed to take longer as well.

She told him about dates to the school's dances, and he felt jealous. But he didn't have the heart to be mad. He hadn't returned for the Fall Dance because he had gotten so focused on transferring—and that probably hurt her. Besides, he had told her to go with Brent.

That, and he never did explain why he left so abruptly. Mother had written him about Mary-Lou's phone call, and he felt terrible to have left without saying anything, but he also wanted to surprise her.

He also didn't want to get her hopes up. He knew he'd get accepted, but he didn't know when they'd allow him to start. It was best to wait until his fate had been decided.

A few weeks before Christmas, one large envelope slid under the door to Randall's bedroom. He had just taken his last exam and was packing to head home for the Christmas break. The large envelope had BYU stamped in the upper corner, and Randall nervously licked his lips as he pulled up the sealed tab. He started to read the letter when a broad smile spread across his face.

Before reading the entire letter, he pushed it back into the envelope and finished packing. He loaded up the Oldsmobile and turned in his dorm key to the landlady. He couldn't stop smiling as he drove home.

His excitement grew as he neared Orem. He first stopped at his home to unload the car, and from the size of his smile, Euveda already knew the contents of the letter. She beamed back at Randall as she ushered him out the door.

As he turned onto Mary-Lou's street, his hands started to sweat, and he grew nervous. A few weeks had passed since either of them had written a letter, and he started to wonder if she was seeing someone else.

But that didn't matter. He had been in love with her for over a year and had never told her. If she had moved on, and didn't feel the same way, he needed to know that.

He walked up to the front door and knocked a few times. Lucinda swung the door open with a smile, but her smile turned upside down as soon as she saw Randall. Without a word, she started to close the door.

But Randall stuck his foot in the door.

"Ugh, Randall," she despitefully gasped. "She's dating other boys. Why don't you just let her be?"

"With all due respect, Mrs. Rawthwort, I'd still like to speak with Mary-Lou. If she doesn't want to see me, I'd like to hear her say that."

Lucinda drew in a deep angry breath through her nose. "Hmmph," she mumbled as she turned back inside the house. Moments later, she returned with Mary-Lou.

A solemn expression hung over Mary-Lou's face. She stepped outside and closed the door behind her, shutting out her mother's prying ears.

"Randall," she said as she nodded. Seeing him there with a hint of a smile reminded her of all the times their conversation and dancing filled her stomach with butterflies. Her eyes dropped to his lips as she remembered their first kiss.

But she forced her eyes away. He probably wasn't here to reciprocate the love she felt—which was for the better. This way she could end it and find some sort of closure.

They exchanged pleasantries before silence settled over them both.

Lucinda peeked through the window, pleased at their visible moods. There was nothing that boy could do to make Mary-Lou smile. She'd come to her senses and pitied the poor boy for having no future.

"I got accepted to BYU," Randall said. He wasn't sure how to say he loved her, but he had to say something.

"Oh, that's nice." Mary-Lou didn't understand why he drove over to share that information. He seemed to expect some excitement from her, but she didn't see what was so exciting?

"Oh, uuh yeah," he stammered. He was crashing hard. He started to rock his foot back and forth. He wanted to leave and end his string of awkward comments, but he was too far in. He had to at least explain why he transferred. But he froze as he gulped down the saliva that watered his mouth.

Mary-Lou waited for some sort of explanation, but Randall didn't seem to have something to add. "Goodnight Randall." She started to head for the door, when Randall called out.

"No, Mary-Lou, you don't get it." He struggled to get his mouth to form the sentences he needed. His body seemed to be conspiring against him as every part wanted to run back to the car.

"I transferred so I could move back here."

She had turned back but felt unimpressed with his explanation. "Rent would be cheaper," she interjected as a matter of fact.

Frustrated that she wasn't piecing his brilliant plan together, he tried again. "I transferred to BYU, so I could move home and be close to *you*. I start in January."

Stunned into silence, her eyes widened. Her heartbeat faster as she started to breathe quickly. Or was it the other way around? Trying to make sense of it all she asked, "But you stopped writing? You told me to date other guys."

Randall stepped closer. He smiled as her reaction replaced his nervousness with the urge to laugh. "Technically, I told you to date Brent."

Her heartbeat only quickened as he stepped closer. His voice was soft and soothing. Why was there no anger or jealousy? She wanted to be mad, but her mind struggled to formulate a counter argument.

"I don't understand," was all she could manage.

Randall let out a small laugh. "I fell in love with you the first time I held you in my arms."

She felt lightheaded. She hadn't expected Randall to be in love with her, especially not for so long. Why had he never said anything? Why had she never said anything?

"But Brent?" Her mind rushed with so many moments as she patched her story with his.

"Orange Daylilies," he said with a shrug. "Brent is as ordinary as they come."

A laugh escaped her lips as she shook her head in disbelief. His confidence suggested that he knew how she felt. He seemed to know any other guy couldn't measure up in her eyes. But her glee stopped short.

"Why didn't you come for the dance?" Her voice conveyed more emotion than she had wanted. She didn't want him to know she was hurt by his absence.

Randall ducked his head as the pain in her voice left his heart aching. "I'm a fool sometimes. I let work and my plan devising supersede you." He closed the gap to Mary-Lou as he wrapped his arm around her waist. "But that's a mistake for the past. From now on, you come first because I love you, Mary-Lou"

Her heartbeat slowed down as Randall tilted his head to the side. He placed his other hand in the middle of her back as he gently pressed his lips against hers. Tears flowed freely down her cheeks as she threw her arms around his neck and kissed him back.

Her tears swept away all the frustration, confusion, and heartache she had bottled up the past few months. Truthfully, they were happy tears because Randall was hers.

An audible gasp came from inside the house. *Mother must have seen the kiss,* she thought. She let out a laugh as she took a step back. They heard a door slam shut, and she guessed mother had just locked herself in the bathroom.

"You know, Mother won't approve," she teased with a gleam in her eye.

Randall wiped away a remaining tear and smiled as he rested his forehead on hers. "I can live with that."

She pulled in close with a whisper. "I love you, Randall Durfey." And she kissed him as he smiled wide. But he stepped back, causing her eyebrows to pull together in confusion.

"One last thing," he said as he reached behind his back and into his back pocket. He pulled out a single orange daylily and gave it to Mary-Lou. With sly smile on his face he met her eye and asked, "Will you go the Christmas Dance with me?"